Ronnie and the Flying Fitted Carpet

Ronnie and the Flying Fitted Carpet

John Antrobus

Illustrated by Rowan Barnes-Murphy

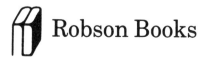 Robson Books

First published in Great Britain in 1993 by Robson Books Ltd,
Bolsover House, 5–6 Clipstone Street, London W1P 7EB

Copyright © 1993 John Antrobus

The right of John Antrobus to be identified as author of this work has
been asserted by him in accordance with the Copyright, Designs and
Patents Act 1988

British Library Cataloguing in Publication Data
A catalogue record for this book is available from the British Library

ISBN 0 86051 822 1

Photoset in Century Schoolbook by
Derek Doyle & Associates, Mold, Clwyd, North Wales.
Printed in Hungary

1

"Welcome to Carpet Kingdom," the plastic gnome at the car-park entrance nodded and bobbed and uttered to every car that went past. "Welcome to Carpet Kingdom. All colours, shapes and sizes fitted to the far reaches of your mind. Be sure that any sort of carpet you require in Carpet Kingdom you will surely find. Never mind, never mind, never mind ..."

An attendant came out and kicked the bobbing gnome.

"Never mind the weather. We will choose a carpet here from those all brought together. Welcome to Carpet Kingdom."

Ronnie liked the plastic gnome. He had been here before. This time his mother wanted a new fitted carpet for the lounge. She drove into a wall and parked the car.

"Did you see that wall move?" she asked Ronnie.

"I don't believe it did," said Ronnie.

"This is a funny place," said Mum. "Let's order our carpet and get out of here. With your imagination, don't you find it spooky?"

Ronnie put his imagination to work immediately. Perhaps the gnome came alive at night and only turned to plastic during the day to lure people in – into Carpet Kingdom, where the carpets ate people. Why not? Some of them looked fierce enough.

DO NOT FEED THE CARPETS, said a sign.

"Oh, that's silly," said Mum. 'The place is full of

gimmicks. All people want to do is buy carpets. They're not here to be entertained."

A clown approached them. He did a handspring on a pile of carpets before producing an order book.

"Can I help you, madam?" he said.

"I'm looking for a carpet to be fitted in my lounge," said Mum.

"We have rolls and rolls of every description, madam. Forward rolls, backward rolls ..." The clown did a backward roll, ending in a handstand. Ronnie applauded.

"We are not here to be entertained, young man," said Mum. "If we wanted this sort of thing we'd go to the circus."

"You wouldn't get a carpet there," said the salesman. "Not at the prices we offer. And look at the amazing variety of colour, texture, patterns ... "

His hand swept towards the astonishing display – there was so much choice it was almost self-defeating.

"Isn't it all too much? Isn't it a bit like me and you?"

The clown sat at a piano and sang:

"Aren't we really just a little like a carpet?
Aren't we really just a little like a rug?
When we're hoovered, brushed and swept.
Don't we feel that we're well kept ...
When we're lying on the floor we like a hug.
Just like a rug.
Just like a rug!"

The manager appeared. "Stop that immediately, Dimple."

"Yes, sir."

"Can't you see that these people want service? They don't require a cabaret."

"Some do, some do," said Dimple.

"I'm very sorry, madam," the manager grovelled. "We do try and please and keep the children entertained while you are about the serious business of buying carpets, but this young man has got his priorities wrong. Dimple, to the stockroom at once."

The forlorn clown, head hung low, dragged his reluctant legs towards the stockroom. Ronnie was sorry to see him go, but Mum was getting so annoyed she would have left if he hadn't.

"And what sort of carpet did madam have in mind?" inquired the manager.

Mum looked at the miles and miles of carpet. "I thought of something brown," she said, "so that when my husband splashes his soup the stains won't show."

"Splashes his soup, does he? The filthy swine!" The manager looked appalled. "He shouldn't be living with you. I should. He doesn't know how to treat a carpet. I do – I'd be good to your carpet. Madam, get rid of your husband and take me for a lodger. That's my advice. Then you can choose any colour carpet you like."

"I can't throw my husband out," said Mum, much to Ronnie's relief. He liked his dad.

"Of course not," smiled the manager. "That was a little joke." He sat down at the piano and started singing:

"Aren't you really just a little like a carpet?
Or a doormat people tread on all day long?
Though you're bashed against the wall,
And never let into the hall,
You still say welcome to all comers as they
        throng ... "

9

He leant across the piano and spoke. "Be fair to yourself. Don't invite everyone you meet to come and wipe their feet on you." And then he continued singing:

"Aren't you really just a little like a carpet,
When all you want to be's a tapestry
That people cherish and adore,
Instead of nailing to the floor?
Oh, isn't this a bit like you and me?"

Mum was so overwhelmed by the sentiment of the song that she sat down on some carpets and took a hanky out.

"You see, we do care at Carpet Kingdom," said the manager sonorously. "And please blow your nose on this carpet sample."

He handed her a free sample.

"Oh, we know ... " He waved his arms airily, nearly knocking Ronnie over. "We know that people come in here bruised and battered, wearied by life, emotionally drained. And it's our job to help them find a carpet that has a meaning for them – at a cheap price – a carpet that refreshes and renews the very spirit."

The clown had crept out again and gone to the piano. Now they both sang:

"And did those feet in ancient time,
Walk upon England's mountains green.
But Heaven knows, they stubbed their toes,
Of Carpet Kingdom they did dream ... "

Ronnie didn't trust the manager, though he liked

the clown. Mum's sales-resistance had completely broken down.

"It would be nice to live here," she said.

"Ah, so many of our customers say that," murmured the manager. "Perhaps one day we'll carpet the world. Then there'll be nothing nasty underfoot."

"Oh, that would be nice," said Mum.

"Thank you," replied the manager.

Mum eventually chose a light-brown carpet with a speckled pattern.

"A very nice choice, madam," said the manager. "Not only will it disguise stains but also it will hide the effects of other food debris trodden into it by your husband."

"Oh, that's very good."

"And even if the cat's sick on it, with this pattern it won't be noticed. We get a lot of demand for this carpet."

Ronnie had wandered off down the vast hall of carpeting. He noticed a roll of carpet tucked away in a corner. It was an amazing shade of green. It really caught the eye. There was something about it. The clown reappeared.

"Don't choose that carpet," he said. "It's flying carpet. Seriously – it comes in rolls these days."

"Is this another of your jokes?" demanded Ronnie.

"No," said the clown. "But I could be wrong. It's what I'm told. We're to discourage the public from buying it – until we can get it grounded. It's a nice colour ... "

"Grounded?" asked Ronnie.

"Well, they say it comes from what used to be Arabia. It's very cheap. It's a job lot. No one knows much about it. Perhaps it doesn't come from Arabia.

I don't know," the clown finished off lamely. The flower in his buttonhole drooped.

Mum found Ronnie. "Come on," she said.

"I've just been looking at that bit of flying carpet, Mum."

Mum instantly fell in love with it. "I must have it," she cried.

"But," said the manager, hurrying over to her, "you've already decided, madam."

"I've changed my mind," she declared. "But what is all this nonsense about it being a flying carpet?"

"Flying carpeting, madam, would be the more correct terminology. We do encourage novelty here. We have squeaking carpeting ..."

The clown tiptoed along some unrolled carpet, and at every step it squeaked.

"That is for fun. We have deep-pile carpet, very deep-pile carpet, and very, very deep-pile carpet!"

The clown demonstrated – up to his ankles in the deep pile, up to his knees in the very deep pile, and up to his waist in the very, very deep pile.

"Of course, we do not get much call for the very, very deep-pile carpet, except up the Amazon, where

they are used to pushing their way through vegetation. We provide machetes as well."

The clown roared like a lion and ran out of the carpet. Ronnie laughed.

"But does this strange green shimmering carpet really fly?" insisted Mum, mesmerized.

"Of course not. We took it to Farnborough for testing in one of the hangars," explained the manager, "because a very funny chap brought it in. A foreigner of the Middle Eastern variety, if I am not mistaken."

"It won't fly without the magic word," said the clown.

"Precisely. But as we don't know what that is, we don't advise people to take the carpet," said the manager.

"I don't believe in magic words anyway," said Mum.

"All words are magic," said the manager. "You can start a war with words. You can also heal people with words. And you can order carpet with words. With words you can make friends and you can make enemies – and you can order more carpet. You can make friends of enemies, and enemies of friends, with words. It all boils down to how much carpet do you want, madam?"

"I want the same amount of carpet in flying green as I originally required in brown."

"Yes, but in brown you had overlap, madam, whereas in flying green – so called – you also have to allow for flap."

"Flap and overlap?" Mum looked perplexed.

"Yes, you have to allow for flap in a flying carpet – flap flap and overlap. So you may not have enough."

"I don't want the carpet to fly," said Mum. "So why

would I want flap flap and overlap? I'll just have overlap."

"That could prove very dangerous at 5,000 feet, madam," said the manager, becoming ponderous. "Overlap won't give you the stability that flap flap would."

"But I do not require the carpet to fly," insisted Mum.

"We'll glue it down as much as we can," said the manager. "In fact, we'll include tap tap. That's overlap, flap flap and tap tap."

"What's tap tap for?" Mum was exasperated.

"To put the nails in." The manager's eyes roamed towards the top of his head and seemed for a moment lost in his eyebrows. "You need overlap, flap flap, tap tap, nap and map."

"Nap and map?"

"Every good carpet has nap. And a flying carpet should have a map. In case you get lost in Arabia."

"I'll have a piece of flying green carpet," said Mum "with overlap, flap flap, tap tap, nap, map and cat."

"Cat, madam?"

"Every good carpet has a cat on it. But we've got a cat already, haven't we, Ronnie?"

"Yes, Mum," said Ronnie.

"Good," said the manager. "Then that's decided. You'll take the brown."

"No, we won't. We'll take the flying green carpet."

"Shall I wrap it up or will you fly it home?" said the manager. "Ha, ha, ha." He laughed at his little joke, as his eyes stared at each other suspiciously across his nose.

The clown stepped forward. "The carpet cannot fly without the magic word," he said. "And no one knows it. Therefore ... "

"Therefore what?" demanded the manager.

"Therefore this carpet should be treated like an ordinary carpet."

"None of our carpets is ordinary, Dimple! How dare you! How dare you demean the very name of Carpet Kingdom! You shall be cast out this very day."

"Where do I pay?" asked Mum.

"At the cash point, madam," declared the manager. "But as for this comedian … " He pointed a trembling finger at the clown. "He shall pay for his heresy until the end of his days … including Thursdays, late night closing, 9 pm, when we offer an enticing 10 per cent discount for all marked items."

He drew a deep breath. "And now let us finish with a little song."

The clown leapt to the piano as if sensing the possibility, at least, of a reprieve, and they sang together:

"Flying green, overlap, flap flap, tap tap.
Flying green, overlap, flap flap, tap tap.
Flying green. Seldom seen. Where's it been? What
    a sheen!
Flying green, overlap, flap flap, tap tap.
Flying green, overlap, flap flap, tap tap.
Nap and map. Nap and cat.
Nip and tuck, lots of luck!
Flying green, overlap, flap flap, tap tap.
Glue it down. Tack it round. Keep it bound to the
    ground.
Keep your windows close and tight.
Watch your carpet day and night.
Mind your language – though absurd,

15

Pray not to use that magic word!
Flying green, overlap, flap flap, tap tap.
Flying green, overlap, flap flap, tap tap.
Flying green. Seldom seen. Where's it been? What
    a sheen!
Nip and tuck. Lots of luck!
Take the map in case you're stuck ...
In Arabia, with flying green ... "

Dimple finished with a flourish. His fingers, like five pounds of reckless sausages flying over the keys, mercifully escaped as the manager slammed down the piano lid.

"Good luck on your journey, madam," he said.

"I'm only going home," said Mum.

"That's not the journey he was talking about," whispered the clown.

2

The carpet had been installed in the lounge for over a week now and Ronnie had been saying magic words over it every spare minute. To no avail: the carpet had not moved. It hadn't lifted. It had not even turned up at the edges. He would jump into the middle of the room, after first opening the window so that the carpet could fly out of the house, and shout "Squoricks!" or some such word. "Alakabam! Squidge!"

"What?" said Dad, waking up from his snooze in front of the TV set.

"Squidge," said Ronnie.

"Oh," said Dad. "We used to eat them when I was abroad." And he fell back to sleep. Later Dad explained to Ronnie that Carpet Kingdom was a shop full of gimmicks and that they would do anything to sell a carpet, including making up stories about flying green.

"If only it were true, Ronnie," he said, "I'd call out the magic word while your mother was in here, having a sit-down, and she could go off to Arabia with the cat." He added, thoughtfully, "Even better, I'd wait till she had her mother around for a cup of tea and I'd shout out the word. Something like 'Vinpaladu!'"

"Did you see the carpet move?" said Ronnie, looking round the room hopefully.

"No," replied Dad. "Not a twitch, worse luck."

That night Ronnie decided to visit Carpet Kingdom. He waited until everyone was asleep, then let himself out of the house. He had an idea to go and ask the plastic gnome for the magic word. Gnomes knew a lot, didn't they? His mind would not let go of the idea that the manager and the clown had been telling the truth, and not just trying to sell carpets in fanciful ways.

He walked and walked. It was quite a long way to the store and he wondered whether he would ever get there. But eventually he saw the gnome bobbing in the moonlight by the car-park entrance. When he got closer Ronnie saw that in reality the gnome was not moving, but that shadows from a nearby tree flitted across it, giving an illusion of movement. The contraption was switched off, so what hope did Ronnie have of the gnome telling him anything? None at all.

"What do you want?" said Ronnie, imitating the gnome's voice.

"I want to know the magic word to make our carpet fly," said Ronnie, speaking in his own voice.

A breeze sighed through the tree. The plastic gnome creaked and moved a fraction of an inch.

"Come on," demanded Ronnie. "Gnomes know all sorts of magic things, don't they?"

"Maybe they do," said the gnome, but it was only Ronnie talking again, doing an impression that he thought might be famous one day.

"Tell me or I'll blow you up!" shouted Ronnie.

"Don't do that," said the gnome.

Ronnie was not sure whether he had used the gnome's voice or not.

"Who said that?"

"I did," said the gnome. "If you don't blow me up

I'll tell you the magic word."

"Go on then," said Ronnie.

"Albusherazam."

"Albusherazam?" repeated Ronnie, wanting to be sure.

The gnome was silent and perfectly still. Its face looked malevolent in the moonlight with that blotchy red grin. Then it was gone. A gust of wind had covered the moon with cloud. In the darkness Ronnie ran home, all the time muttering, "Albusherazam, Albusherazam ... " He wrote the word down before he jumped into bed. Albusherazam. Then he fell into a deep sleep and dreamt he was riding on a carpet.

*

The next morning was a school holiday. Ronnie played well away from the house. Truth to tell, he was scared to go into the lounge in case he said the magic word and flew off on the carpet to Arabia. Perhaps he had imagined it all. Everyone told him he was a very imaginative boy. But he carried round in his pocket, crumpled up on a piece of paper, the word he had found by his bed upon awakening: Albusherazam.

The question was, did the gnome really speak to him, or had he made the whole thing up? He tried the word out on the cat: "Albusherazam". But the cat did not fly away. It obviously only worked on carpets – magic carpets. And possibly only on that particular brand that lay so peacefully in the lounge.

Late that afternoon Ronnie came back to the house. He looked through the open window of the lounge and saw that his mother had laid out tea. His father came in.

"Have you been looking for a job?" asked Mum hopefully.

"No, dear," said Ronnie's dad. "Work finds you soon enough. You don't have to go looking for it." He sat down at the tea-table.

"How are we going to pay the mortgage this month?" asked Mum, biting her lip.

"I don't know, dear. I never was much good at metaphysics."

"It's a job you need," she said.

"It was my last job that led to unemployment," said Dad. "If I had never had it I wouldn't have lost it. Don't worry, dear, something will turn up. Don't take it too seriously. We've bread on the table today. And a new carpet under our feet."

"That was an impulse buy," said Mum sorrowfully.

"It was an act of faith," said Dad. He turned and saw Ronnie in the back garden. "Come in and have your tea, son."

"I'm frightened I'll say the magic word," said Ronnie.

"And what is it today?" inquired his father.

"I'd rather not say," said Ronnie.

"Oh, come on," said his mother. "I wish I'd never taken you to that store. It's all stuff and nonsense. Come in for your tea, Ronnie."

Ronnie approached the french windows. He put one foot into the room, on to the carpet, then drew it back quickly. "I'm sure I've got the right word this time," he said. "Or maybe I haven't. Maybe I made it up and didn't get it from the gnome."

"Just say it through the window, son," said Dad, "and then come in for your tea. There's a good boy."

Ronnie took out the crumpled piece of paper. "All right," he said.

Mum and Dad smiled at him indulgently. How he wished he could help them pay the mortgage.

He cleared his throat and called out, almost apologetically, "Albusherazam."

Carpet tacks began to pop. The floorboards creaked and groaned as the green carpet fought against the glue that held it down. It flapped at the edges and then, as football crowds sometimes do, it did a Mexican wave. Suddenly it was three feet in the air, floating in the lounge. Ronnie watched as the carpet hesitated while getting a sense of direction, then with a whoosh flew out of the house and up into the sky, heading towards Arabia, taking Mum and Dad, the sideboard, the three-piece suite, the table and chairs, the TV and the lamp, and Ginger the cat with it.

Ronnie waited until the speck that was everything previously described had vanished into the East. "It worked," he said. "It must have been the gnome that spoke to me after all." His tea had gone with the carpet. He went into the kitchen to make himself a sandwich, pour a glass of cold milk and ponder his next move.

Ronnie's next move was to go back to Carpet Kingdom.

"No," said the manager. "I don't recall flying green. Do you, Mr Dimple?"

Dimple now stood in the middle of a sad grey suit. "No," he replied.

"And you were dressed as a clown," said Ronnie, almost accusingly.

"Was I?" said Dimple. "Was I really?"

"We are not here to discuss the nature of reality," said the manager. "Or, I might add, our previous promotion weeks. Last week was 'Fun Week'."

"Ho, ho, ho," said Dimple.

"But we must always ring the changes," continued the manager. "This week it's 'Be Reasonable Week', with a lot of sombre grey and deep-brown carpeting."

"Drown, drown, in deepest brown," intoned Dimple. "And fade away in sombre grey."

"Good," said the manager. "Very good, Dimple."

"Oh, careworn life – oh, carefree carpet!" declared Dimple.

"Excellent. Excellent motto, Dimple. Now, where's that boy gone?"

Ronnie ran down the avenues of vulgar carpet displays. He had come to Carpet Kingdom to find a

remnant of flying green. Surely that astonishing magic carpet had not been all used up on furnishing the lounge in his home? If he could get hold of a piece, he could use the magic word and fly after his parents. He ran up and down the ranks of rolled carpeting. There was so much of it — it was like swimming in a soup made of a thousand mixed vegetables.

As he ran and ran he thought about the mortgage. He knew his mother was worried about it, and that his father would like to pay it. And now everyone was involved in a new adventure because of him, and even if his parents did get home, they might not be able to stay there.

"Something will work out, though," said Ronnie, to comfort himself. "It always does."

At that moment his father was watching the snooker on the television as the carpet flew over the Indian Ocean. "Oh, that Jimmy White's good," he said.

"You'd do better to think about how we got up here," said Mum crossly.

"Thinking didn't get us up here and it won't get us down again," said Dad.

Ronnie turned a corner and bumped into the manager.

"What exactly do you want, little boy?" The manager gripped him tightly by the shoulder.

"It's your fault my mum and dad have gone to Arabia with Ginger the cat," puffed Ronnie. "And they've got the telly."

"I didn't send them to Arabia with the telly." The manager smiled, and his brown teeth appeared like old tea-strainers, which is what they were.

"Oh yes you did," said Ronnie. "You sold my mum flying carpet, didn't you?"

"Utter nonsense, balderdash and twaddle," said the manager. "In that order."

"Oh no it's not," said Ronnie. "Because I got the magic word from the gnome."

"Did you now?" The manager looked furious for a moment, then pasted on a smile like a roll of wallpaper over the Grand Canyon. "Mr Dimple," he called. "Kindly escort this bemused young man from the premises."

"*Certainement*," said Dimple, in French, for as a salesman he was ever mindful of the trading possibilities across the Channel.

He led Ronnie out by the hand. As he did so he whispered, "Yes, we did sell you that carpet, of course we did. Flying green. But it was a gimmick. It could not possibly fly."

"Well it did," said Ronnie. "Where's the rest of the roll?"

"It was all used up on your order," said Dimple. "Any small pieces remaining would have been thrown away – sent to the municipal rubbish dump and burnt. Good morning. Have a nice day. *Bonjour*."

Ronnie went home. It was not much fun being on his own. What was he to do? He went down to the local police station.

"*Bonjour*," he said.

"*Bonjour*," said the desk sergeant. "What can we do for you, young fella-me-lad?"

"It's my parents and my ginger cat. They've gone missing," declared Ronnie.

"Oh yes. How did that happen?"

"They flew away on a magic carpet."

"I see. And when did they say they would be returning?"

"They didn't."

"I see." The desk sergeant scratched his ear with a

pencil. "Have you got a registration number for the carpet?"

"No. I used the magic word I got from the gnome," explained Ronnie. "That's why they flew away."

"I see," said the sergeant. "This is very serious. Gnomes giving magic words. Oh dear. They are forbidden to do that, you know. We can't have a lot of carpets flying around. There's enough air traffic already these days."

"Yes," said Ronnie. "Aren't you going to write something down?"

"Well," said the sergeant. "In an important case like this, after a preliminary inquiry, the details should go straight into the computer for missing parents."

Ronnie's eyes widened. "Do you get a lot of missing parents?" he asked.

"Oh yes. We get a lot of parents leaving home these days – running away. We try and trace them and persuade them to go home to their families."

"Good," said Ronnie, much relieved.

"What's your name, son?"

"Bogan. Ronnie Bogan."

"Have you seen a Mr and Mrs Bogan, with a ginger cat? Have they been handed in, Derek?" the sergeant inquired of a pleasant-looking young police constable.

"No, Sergeant. We haven't had any parents handed in today."

The two policemen winked at each other.

"You don't believe me, do you?" said Ronnie, disappointed.

"Take this boy home, Constable," ordered the sergeant. "I want a full investigation. Leave no stone unturned until Ronnie here is restored to his parents."

"OK, Sarge," said Derek, the police constable. "Come on, Ronnie. We'll sort this out, don't worry."

Ronnie liked the young constable. He trusted him. They left the police station together.

"You can hold my hand if you like," said Derek.

"No," said Ronnie. "I don't need to do that."

The policeman stood in the middle of the lounge. "All the furniture is missing," he declared.

"Yes," said Ronnie. "It went out on the flying carpet. As it lifted, the plugs shot out of their sockets but the television stayed on. My father was still watching the snooker as it flew off."

"That would be possible because of the electricity field in and around the carpet," explained Derek.

"So you do believe me," said Ronnie.

"No," replied Derek, "but I'm bringing a logical mind to bear on your story."

They went outside to look around. Derek was intent on finding clues. "If they owed too much on the mortgage they might have upped and left, furniture and all," he said.

"They wouldn't have left me behind." Ronnie's eyes filled with tears.

"I'm sorry. Of course they wouldn't. No, Ronnie, there's got to be another explanation."

"I've given it to you," said Ronnie, or rather he almost shouted it. Just then he spied in a corner by the dustbin a roll of green carpet. There was a letter affixed to it. Ronnie opened the envelope and read:

Dear Customer

I found a small remnant of the carpet you inquired about after all and thought to bring it round. I'm sure it won't fly, but perhaps it will. No, it won't.

Yours sincerely

Monsieur Dimple (the clown)

Ronnie unrolled the carpet.

"Are you coming to Arabia with me?" he asked. "The sergeant said you had to help me find my parents, so you'd better hop on this carpet quick."

Ronnie was standing on the carpet. He was all ready to say the magic word.

"Well?" he demanded. "Are you coming or not? Do you want an adventure?"

Derek did not want to look silly, standing on a remnant of carpet by the dustbins, but it was his duty as an officer of the law to explore all avenues. He stood on the carpet beside Ronnie. "Now what happens?" he said.

Ronnie took out the crumpled piece of paper from his pocket to remind himself of the magic word.

"ALBUSHERAZAM!" he shouted.

The carpet rose and hovered at about three feet from the ground. It was quite firm to stand upon, as

though it had its own gravitational field. Then it slowly swung round until it was orientated towards the East.

"There's still time to jump off," said Ronnie.

"No," said Derek. "I could earn a bit of promotion on a job like this."

The shimmering carpet glowed beneath them, then moved off quickly into the sky towards Arabia.

3

In Arabia a camel burped. It looked up and saw a carpet flying past. Nobody else did.

"I think we've gone past Arabia," said Derek.

"Magic carpets always fly home," said Ronnie.

"This one might not. It could have a flaw in it. It could have gone wrong on the loom – in the weaving. That's why they were selling it off cheap. No guarantee, right? It's silly to buy a bloomin' magic carpet without a guarantee," grumbled Derek. "Especially a magic carpet. We don't even know where it's going now, do we?"

"No," said Ronnie.

The weather was pleasantly warm. They were flying over an ocean, at times so low that flying fish fell on to the carpet. Ronnie threw them back into the sea.

"Anyway," he said, "as long as we're going to the same place as my mum and dad and Ginger."

"Don't count on that," said Derek. "It depends on whether the fault on the loom repeated itself into this end bit – this remnant. It's only a bit cut off, isn't it? It's not what you'd call a proper carpet."

"Well, it answered the magic word, didn't it?" said Ronnie. "The one I got from the gnome."

"Gnomes are very unreliable," continued Derek. "I

wouldn't take a magic word from a gnome. Did he give you a two-year guarantee?"

"What, for the carpet?"

"No, for the magic word."

"No," said Ronnie. "I didn't think to ask."

"There you are. No book of instructions. No guarantee. Never buy an electrical appliance from a gnome."

"This isn't an electrical appliance," answered Ronnie. "It's a magic carpet."

"It has an electrical field," stated Derek, "that works by Ohm's Law."

"It could work by Gnome's Law," said Ronnie. He was not very happy with the thought that he might not be able to rescue his parents after all. He and Derek might be going anywhere. Oh, well. He fell asleep and dreamt he flew on a magic carpet low over an ocean among a shoal of flying fish. They turned colder, to ice, as they tumbled on to the flying carpet. Ronnie tried to scoop the frozen fish back

31

into the sea but they were too heavy, weighing the carpet down dangerously near to the wave tops. A gigantic wave loomed up ahead.

"Watch out!" shouted Derek, and Ronnie woke up.

Ahead of them was a mountain. The carpet skimmed up through an icy blizzard and over the peak. Yet more mountains faced them, stretching higher and higher. Derek took out his truncheon and tried to bash the icicles off the edge of the carpet.

"ALBUSHERAZAM!" shouted Ronnie, to encourage the carpet. It shook, vibrating violently, and the ice miraculously fell off. Free of the weight, the carpet sped upwards and wove its way between the peaks and glaciers below.

"Hurrah!" shouted Ronnie.

The carpet began to descend. The weather grew warmer. The mountains lay behind them. Beneath them was a valley, lush and verdant.

They landed in a quiet green field. The tinkling of yak bells greeted them.

A monk came up to them. His smile was quite infectious. It spread right across his face, stopped only by his ears. "Have you come to have a look at the zoo?" he asked.

"Yes, please," said Ronnie.

"This way then." The monk cheerfully led them further down into the valley.

Derek took out his notebook. He coughed. "And what might be the name of this place?"

"Shangri-La," answered the monk. "Everyone stays young here for ever. It's very boring."

"Shangri-La." Derek laboriously wrote it down in his notebook. "Yes, I've heard of this place. Do you get a lot of juvenile crime?"

"It's possible," answered the monk, as he strode

along. "The trouble is there's so much of everything here it's not worth stealing."

"Oh dear." Derek didn't like the thought of that. "Don't you ever get old ladies who have their handbags snatched?"

"I expect we would if we had old ladies. But, as I said, we don't have any old people here. Except, that is ... " The monk turned to face them. His eyes twinkled as he continued walking backwards. "Except in the zoo. You might find a couple of old ones there. Of course, they're kept in their own atmosphere."

Ronnie was listening to the conversation, but also he could not help noticing the profusion of meadow flowers that spread around them. They were

33

beautiful. "Does anyone ever pick the flowers?" he asked.

"Oh, no," said the monk. "That's a crime."

"I might be able to help there." Derek looked hopeful.

Ronnie, who was walking along with the bit of carpeting rolled up under his arm, thought about what the monk had said.

"Do you really keep people in a zoo?" he asked.

"Of course," said the monk. "Doesn't everybody? It is forbidden to feed them. Be warned before we get there."

They came to an entrance, and met an old friend – the bobbing plastic gnome.

"Welcome to the People Zoo!
Here we keep them two by two.
Selected from the world at large.
Have you any questions, Sarge?"

"I'm not a sergeant," said Derek. "But, yes, I have. How long have you been a gnome?"

"For ever."

"Are you naughty?"

"Sometimes I might be, but only for fun."

"And what is your idea of fun?"

"Being naughty."

"That's the same gnome that was outside Carpet Kingdom. He gave me the magic word," declared Ronnie.

"Ah ha," said Derek, which he always said when he could not think of anything else to say.

"Come along," said the monk. "This way."

They entered the zoo through an arch and walked down a path.

"This is Exhibit One," said the monk. They stood before a transparent dome. Inside it a room was set out and in it sat two people – a man and a woman. They were watching television. "They're from Holland," said the monk, and led them round a corner to another exhibit.

"This pair are from Uganda." Inside this dome sat another man and woman, watching television.

There were a few other visitors to the zoo, locals obviously, who were only mildly curious about the exhibits they had come to see. The monk seemed eager to move on with Ronnie and Derek.

"Come on, come on," he said pleasantly, and bustled them on.

There were other domes with other room settings and other couples to look at. Though the furnishings were sometimes more like a bedroom than a lounge, the one thing they all had in common was a TV set. And in every dome the couple were watching the TV.

"Is that all they do? Watch the telly?" said Ronnie.

"Apparently," said the monk. "It's something we don't have, and it's hard to explain, but that's what they do. We have a Shangri-La satellite to beam in all the programmes."

There were domes with couples from all over the world, labelled China, Russia, Mongolia, Germany, Canada, USA, Scotland, Iceland, Uruguay, Brazil, Estonia, Latvia, France, Belgium ... Ronnie and Derek were shown them all.

"And here's our latest exhibit," said the monk. "We're very pleased with this one. It's got a cat as well. That's very rare."

Inside a dome were Ronnie's mum and dad, watching the TV, with Ginger the cat. Ronnie waved and called, "Mum! Mum! Dad! Dad!" but he got no response.

"They can't hear you," said the monk. "They are quite sealed off. But very happy. We look after them. We feed them. And in the rarefied atmosphere we provide they will last for ever as well, and not age any more. Think of that."

"Do they grow younger?" asked Ronnie.

"Not much," replied the monk, smiling vaguely. "Do you happen to know these people?"

"No, he doesn't," said Derek quickly. "He often jumps up and down saying, 'Mum, Mum, Dad, Dad', don't you, Ronnie?"

"Yes," said Ronnie. As they moved on he jumped up and down, shouting, "Mum! Mum! Dad! Dad!"

They came to a building marked REGIS-TRATION. They entered and found another monk, who smiled as much as the first one, sitting behind a counter. "I'll be leaving you now," said the first monk. As he left, a metal grille descended behind him, cutting off the way out for Ronnie and Derek.

Derek said, "Oi! Hang on. I don't like that."

"Just a precautionary measure." The seated monk beamed at them both. "In case you're dangerous."

"We're not dangerous," said Derek.

"Good," said the monk. "Jolly good. What's your favourite food?"

"Strawberries and ice-cream," said Ronnie.

"I'll make sure you get lots of that," said the jolly monk.

"Beefburgers and chips," said Derek.

"Right you are. Lovely." The happy monk smiled as though the world could not have given him a brighter day. "Now, did you bring any furniture with you?"

"No," said Ronnie.

"And you arrived on that bit of carpeting?" The monk indicated the rolled-up piece of magic carpet under Ronnie's arm.

"Yes," said Ronnie.

The monk looked a bit perplexed. "You arrive on a remnant of carpet with absolutely no furniture and expect to be accepted by the zoo?"

"No," said Derek.

"Yes," said Ronnie. He thought that while they were here there was a chance to rescue Mum and Dad. He didn't want them staying in Shangri-La for ever, watching television. Even the cat had ignored him. And what was the good of them staying young for ever? That meant one day he would be older than them. Mind you, they weren't that young, his parents. But they might start asking for pocket money – you never knew!

"The problem is," said the monk, regaining his sunny disposition, "and I'm sure we can work this out together – we have no idea of your natural environment. And we do like to place our specimens in exactly the environment they came from."

"Oh," said Derek, disappointed, for he had a rather small room in Paddington. "Well, I come from Buckingham Palace."

"And I come from a room like the one belonging to those recent specimens you've got in," said Ronnie.

"You can't go in with them," said the monk firmly. "All new arrivals are screened for suitability, placed in their own environment, or released back into the wild." He punched the details he had into a computer. "Well, we'll let you know soon enough. Till then we'll put you in quarantine."

"Oh no you won't," said Derek, and tried to jump across the desk, but he hit an invisible screen and bounced back.

"So you *are* dangerous," said the monk amiably. "You'll soon settle down with your favourite TV programmes, and lots of strawberries and ice-cream and beefburgers."

"And chips," added Derek, picking himself up off the floor.

"And chips."

"And tomato ketchup," said Derek.

"Right-ho," smiled the monk, adding the extra information into the computer. "Just wait here, will you?" He touched a button, a panel opened and through he went.

Ronnie unrolled the piece of carpeting and stood on it. "Get on," he said to Derek. "This magic carpet will sail through anything."

Derek stepped on to the carpet.

"ALBUSHERAZAM!" shouted Ronnie. Nothing happened.

Derek stepped off the carpet. "It won't work 'cos

that was the magic word to get us here, and now we're here we're stuck," he said miserably.

All they could do was wait, so Derek sang "The Policeman's Waiting Song". He had a fine tenor voice. He removed his helmet and gave forth:

"A policeman has to wait
Outside the Palace gate
And by a scene of crime
He likes to bide his time
A cry or an alarm
Means he could come to harm
Much better then to wait
Outside that Palace gate
While tourist cameras click
He bends his knees – but not too quick
On foreign photographic plates
Smiles our policeman, as he waits
Behind him etched those Palace gates
With Queen in window, she in State
Oh pity our policeman's fate
For 'tis his lot to stand and wait ..."

"Did you enjoy that?" asked Derek, placing his helmet back upon his head with unerring accuracy.

"Yes, thank you," replied Ronnie. "I was practising not listening, like I do at home when mum and dad argue."

"Oh," said Derek. "Thank you."

4

Ronnie and Derek were duly installed under a dome and the small piece of carpeting was put in with them. The Inspector of Zoos was brought along.

"This won't do at all," he said. "They've got no telly."

"No," said a monk. "They didn't bring one."

"Well, send them back. They've got no furniture either. These are very poor specimens." The Inspector was not impressed.

Ronnie strained to hear what they were saying.

"They want to send us home," he whispered. "Because we're poor specimens."

"In that case they must have the means to do so," pondered Derek. "Like another magic word, for instance."

Ronnie put his ear against the glass-like substance of the dome and thus he could hear all they were saying outside.

"The gnomes are responsible for sending us good specimens," said the Inspector.

"That's right," said a monk. "They make sure our carpeting is sold all over the world."

"And then?" inquired the Inspector. "Then what happens?"

"We told you yesterday," said another monk.

"Well tell me again today. It's my favourite story," said the Inspector. He put his thumb in his mouth.

"Then, when the magic carpeting is laid out in the homes, a gnome goes round – usually at night – and utters the magic word ... "

"He must make sure a window's open first," said another monk.

"Then the carpet flies away to Shangri-La with all the contents aboard, including people."

"That is a lovely story," said the Inspector. "We have the best People Zoo in the world. We have the only People Zoo in the world. We must continue to collect the very best specimens from all over, in as much variety as possible, before the rest of the world dies."

Ronnie's eyes widened. He could not believe what he was hearing. The people of Shangri-La expected the rest of the world to die, while they lived on for ever! And meanwhile they amused or educated themselves by visiting the People Zoo, where they had had the foresight to gather specimens from all over the world, including two Eskimos who had been sold some carpeting for their igloo – that proved how clever the gnomes were!

The Inspector for Zoos pointed at Ronnie and Derek. "They are substandard. WHAT ARE YOU SMILING ABOUT?"

"We are the Smiling Monks," they said. "We always smile."

"But this is no smiling matter. Send them back immediately," he ordered. "Find a gnome who has the magic word to do it. That's what gnomes are for, isn't it?"

"Yes, yes," agreed the Smiling Monks.

Having delivered his verdict, the Inspector returned to his office. The Smiling Monks obediently went off to look for a gnome.

Back in the dome, Derek said cheerfully, "We don't

We always smile......

need to wait for a bloomin' gnome to send us home.
They're always unreliable. I've worked out the magic
word myself."

He tore out a page from his notebook and gave it to
Ronnie. On it was written "Mazarehsubla".

"It's Albusherazam spelt backwards," said Ronnie.

"It's easy to say that now," said Derek, who had felt
quite pleased with himself.

"I'm not saying you're not clever," said Ronnie.
"But the point is, we don't want to go home without
the others. That's why we came here."

"An investigation is one thing," said Derek. "But

making an arrest is another. We really need the van."

"We haven't got the van," said Ronnie. "And you can't expect them to drive from the Harrow Road Police Station to Shangri-La. Anyway, how do we know this word 'Mazarehsubla' will work?"

Immediately the bit of magic carpeting flew to the top of the dome. It pressed so strongly against it that the dome began to lift off the ground. Seizing the opportunity, Ronnie and Derek rolled out under the lip of the dome.

Ronnie shouted, "Albusherazam!" and the carpet fluttered back to the ground. The dome jarred back into place. Ronnie and Derek were outside it, the carpet lay peacefully within.

"That was a bit of quick thinking," said Derek.

They walked out of the zoo without being recognized by anybody as escaping specimens.

As they made their way up the valley the sound of bells drew them to a temple.

"In 'ere," said Derek, and they ducked through a small low door at one side of the building. Inside, the first thing that Ronnie noticed was the smell of incense. It reminded him of the piece of flying carpet. As his eyes became accustomed to the gloom, he saw why – there were dozens of monks sitting cross-legged on the floor, working at individual looms. At one end of the temple he saw a huge roll of flying green. Somehow they managed to take all these individual magic carpets and stitch them invisibly into a roll of carpeting, so that the unsuspecting public would not guess the origins of their purchase.

An abbot bore down upon them, beaming. He was obviously of the Order of Smiling Monks. "Are you the escapees?" he chuckled. "Make yourselves at home. Feel free to wander where you like."

"Isn't the Inspector of Zoos after us?" asked Ronnie.

"No, the man's a bungler. A fool. He has such a sense of self-importance that we had to give him a job to satisfy his vanity. It's of little consequence. Inspector of Zoos, indeed. He has no jurisdiction outside the zoo, and little in it."

"He sent the monks to fetch a gnome to send us home," said Ronnie.

"Don't tell him everything," said Derek.

But Ronnie was usually right when he trusted somebody, and also when he did not.

"Getting home is not as easy as you imagine," said the Abbot. "Couldn't you make yourself comfortable here in Shangri-La?"

"In the zoo?" said Ronnie.

"I'm not in favour of all that," replied the Abbot vaguely. "I'd rather let you roam around in some sort of park."

"With a boating pond?" suggested Derek.

"What a good idea. Come and have some tea."

The Abbot led them to a low table, and they all squatted round it. A herb tea that was most pleasant to taste was served and cakes that tasted of coconut.

"That old-style zoo place has got to go," said the Abbot. "The theory is that unless you specimens have your own special atmosphere in the domes, you'll grow old and demoralize us all."

"Why?" demanded Derek.

"Because you have the habit of it," answered the Abbot. "But I think the opposite. Here in Shangri-La it's so tranquil and peaceful, I'm sure the effects would rub off on anyone."

He got up to go.

"Oh, by the way," he said. "Feel free to roam around, but keep out of the way of any gnomes. They are mischievous little blighters."

"What if we want to go back to the zoo?" asked Ronnie.

"Put on the habit of a monk," said the Abbot, "and none will dare to stop you." He left them to finish their tea and cakes.

"You trust people too easily," said Derek.

"No, I don't," said Ronnie. "I can tell."

"Perhaps that's my problem then," said Derek. "I never can tell. That's why I'm a policeman."

46

Ronnie fetched two monks' habits from among several hanging on neat wooden pegs on the wall. They put them on, and started smiling.

"We are now in the Order of Smiling Monks," declared Derek, as they left the temple.

As sunset approached they saw lots of people heading towards the zoo.

"What's so special about tonight?" said Derek.

They went closer to have a look. They saw the gnome at the entrance, bobbing and uttering to all and sundry:

"Welcome to the People Zoo,
Watch them dancing, two by two ...
Can-can, Samba, and Fandango,
Foxtrot, Rumba, Waltz and Tango."

Ronnie and Derek pulled up the cowls of their habits to cover their faces and entered the zoo unnoticed – they hoped.

Once inside it became clear that the festivities centred around the specimens. Every evening they danced for their supper. As this was the only time they did anything other than watch TV, it explained why the People Zoo was deserted until sunset.

As the sun went down, the music began to play and in each dome a dance tune particular to the nationality of the inmates could be heard.

Ronnie wanted to see his mum and dad dance. He could not remember ever having seen them do so before. He and Derek arrived just in time. The music

47

was playing a waltz, "Save the Last Dance for Me".
Dad was dressed in tails and Mum had on a
ballroom frock that was quite splendid. With the
numbers pinned to their backs they looked like a
couple in *Come Dancing*, a TV programme Ronnie
had once seen. So glamorous! As they glided round
the floor, or rather over the green carpeting, they
looked very happy. The people outside were
clapping, and Ronnie was glad for his parents. I
cannot take them away from all this, he thought, to
face so many difficulties back home. Perhaps they
liked it here at the People Zoo, where they could live

for ever, and dance every night in Shangri-La.

A thunderclap sounded and lightning flashed. Clouds had gathered in the sky from nowhere. Dad, with a flourish, guided Mum over towards where Ronnie stood outside the dome. "Can you get us out?" he mouthed, before they danced away to the opposite side of the dome in an intricate series of fishtails, to renewed applause.

Ronnie said to Derek, "Come on. They want to come home after all."

"Who do?" said Derek.

"My mum and dad. They haven't become stupefied living here. They want to go home and pay the mortgage. Come *on!*"

"Where are we going?" asked Derek.

"You'll see."

As another crack of thunder rolled across the valley and lightning flashed again, Ronnie led the way towards a large building marked ADMINISTRATION.

Derek said, "The problem is, how do we get the magic word inside the dome to all the inmates."

"*Specimens,*" corrected Ronnie. "I've got the answer to that."

"And even if you give them the magic word there's no knowing they're going to want to use it."

"We don't give the inmates the magic word," said Ronnie.

"*Specimens,*" corrected Derek.,

"Yes," said Ronnie. "We give it to the carpet."

"Carpeting," corrected Derek.

They went inside the building. It was deserted. Everyone was outside watching the dancing.

"This way," said Ronnie, and ran down a corridor. He did not know where he was going and yet he knew it was the right way. Yes, there was a door marked MUSIC. Ronnie burst in. Derek trailed after him.

Inside the room spools revolved silently on different machines, sending the various dance tunes to all the different domes. It looked very efficient. Ronnie threw a switch labelled AUTOMATIC to MANUAL, and picked up a microphone. He knew intuitively what to do.

'MAZAREHSUBLA!" he shouted, and then raced outside with Derek to see the effect.

The domes were taking off into the sky, powered by the green carpeting under each one of them.

"They're going home," shouted Ronnie.

"What about us?" said Derek.

The specimens in their dance costumes looked surprised as they rose up. Some of them waved at the crowd below. The people of Shangri-La had been nice to them in their own way – feeding them, making sure they had television programmes, and providing them with wonderful dance costumes, made to order. It was clear a few of them did not want to go home, but there was nothing they could do about it.

There was one dome that had not taken off. That was the dome previously inhabited by Ronnie and Derek. Being empty, no music had been piped into it that evening. Indeed the PA system was switched off. Even if the bit of carpeting had responded to the magic word, it was not big enough to lift the dome very far. Yet however small it was, it was upon this piece of carpeting that Ronnie and Derek now fixed their hopes. They ran through the zoo towards the solitary dome.

In front of them stood a gnome. The same gnome? Another gnome? They did not know. It started to speak:

"Welcome now to Shangri-La ...
Though you plan to travel far
And go from us, it isn't right,
Please be advised to stay tonight."

They ran past the creature, who repeated, "to stay tonight, to stay tonight, to stay tonight ... "

"It's stuck," said Ronnie.

"I don't care," said Derek. "As long as we're not stuck."

When they reached the dome Derek took out his truncheon and struck the transparent surface repeatedly. But it did not shatter like glass.

"Hurry up," said Ronnie.

"It won't break." Derek tried again.

Down the valley Ronnie could see the other domes in the sky heading towards the mountains. It was just as well that each carpet and its owners were protected by a dome, because they were now flying into the black clouds of the storm.

The gnome suddenly appeared and, using a remote control, obligingly activated a sliding panel, so that Ronnie and Derek could simply walk into the dome. This they did and the panel shut behind them. The gnome looked triumphant.

"I'm not sure this is a good idea," said Derek.

"How else are we going to escape with the others?" demanded Ronnie. "We've got to trust our piece of carpet."

They looked at it, lying there. It was magic, to be sure, and had brought them this far. But it was only a small piece of carpeting and could surely not carry the dome away over the mountains as those other, bigger pieces of magic carpeting were doing right now.

"MAZAREHSUBLA!" shouted Ronnie.

The carpet rose about three feet, but did not fly immediately to the top of the dome. Instead, it upended itself and spun round like a drill, powering into the ground. Earth spattered out from under it. A hole appeared, and then a tunnel. Ronnie could see the gnome outside, jumping up and down in a fury.

"Come on," said Derek.

They crawled into the tunnel, and were soon outside the dome. The carpet, the beautiful piece of magic carpeting, waited for them like a trusty steed, hovering about a foot above the ground.

Round the other side of the dome Ronnie could hear the gnome creaking and squeaking, "To stay tonight, to stay tonight, to stay tonight ... " It was stuck again!

They jumped on to the magic carpet. Without another word, for it needed no bidding, the carpet took off into the sky, leaving the People Zoo far below, and the receding figure of the bobbing gnome.

They flew up the valley towards the mountains. Although sheet lightning seemed to bar their way, the magic carpet sailed through it with no problem. But then suddenly it lost height and began to fall below the storm, which swirled away across the mountains. They landed quietly on a hillside.

*

"This moth-eaten piece of stuff has short-circuited," complained Derek, stepping off the carpeting in disgust. "I told you never to buy electrical equipment from a gnome!"

"What's happened?" Ronnie asked, gazing down at the forlorn piece of green mat that lay before them on the slope. It seemed to have lost all its magical properties.

"The carpet's electrical field became confused in the storm," explained Derek. "It blew out. It fused ... and there ain't no bloomin' fuse box, is there?"

"No," agreed Ronnie. He'd never heard of a carpet with a fuse box. "Can't you mend it?"

"Mend it? I wouldn't know where to start."

Derek went to kick the carpeting, but thought better of it. "We'll just have to wait until someone comes along."

"No one's going to come along," said Ronnie. "All the others have gone home."

"That's right," replied Derek miserably. "If you had got a guarantee for this absurd piece of paraphernalia, we could have taken it back."

"We can't take it back because it doesn't fly," said Ronnie.

"If it flew, we wouldn't need to take it back," said Derek.

"Then how will we ever get out of Shangri-La?" demanded Ronnie.

"That's a good question," replied Derek. "All we need is a good answer."

They were on their own. There might well be a lot of angry local people down below in the valley, feeling cheated about their zoo and planning to come looking for them. And it was getting dark.

5

They slept that night in a cave. The next morning it was fair and sunny, and soon it became warm. For breakfast they picked mushrooms and cooked them over a fire of pine cones.

"Let's try again," said Ronnie.

They stood on the carpet and Ronnie shouted out, "MAZAREHSUBLA." The magic carpeting did not move. He tried several times more, but to no avail.

"Come on, we'll have to walk," said Derek.

Ronnie picked up the carpet and rolled it up. He put it under his arm and followed his companion.

"Why are you bringing that stupid bit of green stuff?" grumbled Derek.

"I like this carpet," said Ronnie. "It's magic ... "

"It's not magic any more!"

"It might be having a rest," said Ronnie.

They walked round the edge of the valley, keeping to the hillsides to avoid any people down below who might be blaming them for all sorts of things.

"Where are we going?" asked Ronnie, as they toiled along.

"I thought you knew," said Derek.

"No, I'm following you," said Ronnie.

"Well, I'm following you," replied Derek.

They sat down on a rock, after first drinking water from a stream. Derek had used his helmet to do that.

"Useful things, helmets," he said vaguely. "You can put a lot in a helmet."

"Yes, you can put your head in it," said Ronnie. After a moment he added, "I thought we were going to the temple to get another piece of carpeting."

"That's what I thought," said Derek. "What a coincidence."

They stood up and continued on their way.

They knew something was wrong when they saw smoke rising above the ridge they were climbing. The Abbot appeared, coming to meet them.

"Good morning," he said. "The temple burnt down last night. Struck by lightning. It couldn't have happened at a better time."

"Why's that?" inquired Derek, taking out his notebook.

"Because everything happens at the right time," replied the Abbot. He beamed at them, his smile radiant.

"Shangri-La is doomed," he declared. "It's wonderful news. Come and have some tea."

As they followed the Abbot, Ronnie whispered to Derek, "Why is it wonderful news?"

The Abbot heard him and answered, "Because we don't believe in bad news here. It's too depressing."

He led them to a clearing among some pine trees. Smiling Monks served them tea from a big cauldron.

"Have you heard the good news? We're doomed. We're doomed," they said.

"Congratulations," said Derek.

"We want to go home," said Ronnie. "Can you help us?"

"Certainly," said the Abbot. "Home is wherever you happen to be. Does that make you feel better?"

"Yes, thank you," said Ronnie. "I was wondering whether there was any of that carpet left over from the fire at the temple?"

"At a reduced price," interjected Derek. "A 'Fire Sale'."

"Oh, you can have what we've got for nothing," said the Abbot.

"What have you got?" inquired Derek.

"Nothing," said the Abbot.

"And a lot of it," said one of the Smiling Monks, smiling.

*

56

A big book was brought forward. This at least – and this at most, it seemed – had been saved from the fire. The Abbot opened the book, selected a page and read: "The First Prophecy of Doom. A desire for entertainment, signalling a restlessness of spirit, shall lead to the destruction of Shangri-La."

The Abbot put the ancient book aside. "The People Zoo. The idea of it was the first infection."

He read on: "The Second Prophecy of Doom. The temple shall be burnt down, and the making of magic carpets shall cease."

The Smiling Monks clapped. Anything made them happy, which is how they stayed happy.

"These are signs of what is to come," announced the Abbot, and continued "The Third Prophecy of

Doom. The microbe cometh and all shall turn to dust."

"It's true," said a monk, smiling broadly. He sneezed, and disappeared, turning to dust in front of them. The powder drifted away towards the ground.

"Did you see that?" said Ronnie.

"Yes, that's another one gone," said the Abbot. "Try not to sneeze, there's good chaps. There's only a dozen of us left now. And we've still got some tidying up to do."

Derek was still taking notes. "What about all the Shangri-Larians down in the valley?" he inquired.

Another monk sneezed and disappeared in a cloud of dust. The others formed a smaller group, jostling together happily.

"Oh, the people down in the valley will have disappeared quicker than we have," explained the Abbot. "Were you trying to avoid them? There's no one left to avoid. Once the microbes got out of those dome atmospheres and into the air of Shangri-La it was curtains for everybody. Not that we use curtains," he added. "They collect dust."

At the thought of dust two more monks sneezed. "Atishoo! Atishoo!" And that was two more gone.

"Why didn't they catch the microbes when the people on the carpets first arrived?" asked Derek cleverly. "They were in contact with them."

"Yes," the Abbot deliberated. "Perhaps they did. It's all in the mind. The prophecies had to come true. We all believe in them. People in Shangri-La have lived happily for hundreds and hundreds of years, until eventually – oh dear – they grew tired of it. Everybody likes a change, don't they?"

"Yes," said Ronnie. "I'd like a change. I'd like to go home."

While the Smiling Monks tidied up the camp site, Ronnie and Derek went to inspect the ruins of the temple, still smouldering in the morning sunlight.

"I suspect arson," stated Derek. "A cursory glance at the evidence suggests the fire was started in three separate places."

The Abbot appeared beside them. He looked upset. "I confess that we burnt down the temple," he said, "so that when we disappeared our secrets of magic-carpet making would disappear with us."

Derek took out his notebook. "I should warn you that anything you say may be taken down and used in the Police Concert," he said.

"That's all right by me," responded the Abbot. "I'm glad to get this off my chest."

He took off a woollen vest that he was wearing.

"That's better," he said. "And another thing, the gnomes are still down there in the valley. As they are made of plastic, the microbes cannot destroy them. They will be up here presently, but they will find nothing."

"How did they get the magic words to activate the carpets?" asked Derek.

"We trusted one of the gnomes and he told the others," said the Abbot.

"Oh, you should never trust a gnome," scolded Derek.

"It does not matter," replied the Abbot. "For all things have worked to fulfil the prophecies of the end of Shangri-La."

Ronnie noticed a pool in the middle of the temple floor. In it was a strange liquid, green and shimmering, which reminded him of his piece of carpeting. With a flash of insight, he realized that this pool had magic properties. He took his remnant and dipped it in the pool. Immediately the carpet began to glow and the sheen was restored to it.

"The carpet's got back its magic properties," shouted Ronnie. "Come on, let's get aboard and go home."

"Yes," said the Abbot. "That's the magic pool, and now you can catch the last piece of carpet out of Shangri-La."

Ronnie and Derek jumped on to the carpet. It would be foolish to waste time in case anything else went wrong.

"Goodbye! Goodbye!" they both shouted. All the Smiling Monks ran to the temple to wave them off.

"Goodbye! Goodbye!" they called out.

"MAZAREHSUBLA!" shouted Ronnie.

The carpet rose and swirled, stirring up a cloud of

dust. All the Smiling Monks were caught in it; they sneezed and immediately disappeared. As the dust subsided only the Abbot remained.

"Goodbye," he called out, waving in a very dignified manner.

The carpet soared up into the sky. Ronnie and Derek waved at the receding figure of the Abbot. No doubt he had such self-control that he did not have to sneeze, but now that everyone else was gone, sneeze he surely would when he was good and ready. And that would be the end of Shangri-La, now a malevolent place, crawling with plastic gnomes. But who cared?

"Let's have one more look at the valley, and see if we can see any of those nasty gnomes," suggested Ronnie.

"I don't know if that's a good idea," said Derek.

But the carpet had heard Ronnie's words and it dived towards the valley. Yes, there were the gnomes. How angry they were, waving their fists and turning their blotchy red cheeks skywards, while they squeaked in indignation. And how Ronnie laughed at their frustration.

"Come on, let's get out of here," said Derek. "Before something goes wrong. Don't push your luck."

Once more the carpet swooped low over the gnomes, then they headed out of the valley. The sport was over.

"That was fun," said Ronnie.

But the fun was not over yet. For, still flying quite low, the carpet snagged on a bramble bush. A thread got caught upon it and it unravelled very quickly. Ronnie and Derek jumped and fell upon the hard ground of Shangri-La. The carpet was no more. A long thread stretched back to the bramble bush. Other shorter threads lay scattered along the pathway of their disastrous descent. And the gnomes were coming.

Ronnie and Derek ran into the forest of pines. In and out among the trees and across sunlit glades they ran, until at last they could run no more. They collapsed in a heap.

"I don't think they followed us," gasped Derek, panting for breath.

"No," said the Abbot, emerging from behind a rock. "Gnomes are notoriously lazy. They will have a pow-wow now, and decide what to do. Which means they will fall asleep for a little while. They never like climbing up hillsides in the heat of the day."

"How do you know what happened?" asked Ronnie.

"I saw it all," chuckled the Abbot. "We're quite near the edge of the forest here. You've been running round in circles."

"Can't you help us?" begged Ronnie. "Please."

"Well, it so happens I can," said the Abbot, beaming hugely. "I knew I was not meant to sneeze yet awhile. There was one more thing for me to do at Shangri-La. Look." He went back behind the rock and brought out a loom.

"I saved this from the fire," he explained. "If you go and fetch the threads, perhaps I can weave the carpet together again."

"Hurrah!" shouted Ronnie.

"But don't wake up the gnomes," warned the Abbot. "Made of plastic, they cannot sweat, and they get very irritable if woken up in the heat of the day."

Ronnie and Derek crept out of the forest and back down the hillside. Ronnie found the end of the thread and started winding it up into a ball as he went further and further down the hill. Meanwhile, Derek picked up all the other threads he could find. As they approached the bramble bush, they came upon gnomes lying around everywhere, fast asleep in the shade of rocks. Their mouths were open, and some of them snored, making squeaking noises at the same time. Ronnie wanted to laugh but he dared not, as they tiptoed past. They reached the bramble bush. Ronnie detached the thread. They crept back past the gnomes and were soon once again in the safety of the forest.

"Well done," said the Abbot, and threaded up the loom with great dexterity. He began weaving the carpet to make it new again.

"It will probably come out quite a bit smaller," he told them.

"Never mind," said Ronnie. "As long as we can get on it."

The Abbot worked through the afternoon, and though he wove with much speed and skill, the two fugitives wondered whether the magic carpet would be ready before the gnomes woke and renewed the chase.

Derek went to the edge of the forest. He came back and reported gloomily, "The gnomes are awake."

"I'm going as fast as I can," said the Abbot cheerfully. "I'm sure it will be ready in time."

"What do gnomes do," asked Ronnie, "if they catch you?"

"Tease you unmercifully," said the Abbot.

Ronnie did not like to be teased. Time was passing. Derek went to the edge of the forest again. He came back, running this time.

"The gnomes are coming," he called out.

"I've nearly finished. Don't worry," declared the Abbot.

"That carpet is our only hope," said Ronnie.

"Do you think so?" The Abbot looked serious for a moment. He cut the carpet, now much smaller, from the loom. "Do you know the magic word?" he asked.

"Of course we do," said Ronnie.

"So do I," said the Abbot, with a very broad smile. The gnomes had reached the trees.

"MAZAREHSUBLA!" shouted the Abbot. The carpet rose from the ground. Its magic powers had not been impaired.

"Quick, let's hop aboard," called out Derek.

"MAZAREHSUBLA!" shouted the Abbot, a second time.

"Wait! Wait!" shouted Derek.

Derek and Ronnie scrambled up towards the carpet. The carpet had moved higher still at the second command.

"Get on that rock and jump, Ronnie," directed Derek.

They scrambled up upon a rock which fortunately lay beside the floating carpet.

"MAZAREHSUBLA!" shouted the Abbot, and the carpet flew away, leaving Ronnie and Derek behind.

"What did you do that for?" asked Derek, dismayed and indignant.

The Abbot smiled beatifically, and then explained. "Your friend Ronnie said that your only hope lay with a miserable piece of carpeting."

"What's wrong with that?" demanded Derek.

"It wasn't ordinary carpet, it was magic," accused Ronnie. "And now you've sent it home without us."

"The only real magic is in your mind, Ronnie," declared the Abbot. "That's what will get you home. Don't put your hopes on things external. Rather, you should trust the *Invisible*. It's from there all things come into your life ... and it's to there all things must return."

The Abbot's smile was larger than that of the renowned Cheshire Cat, and like that cat, after pinching his nose and producing a tremendous sneeze, he disappeared – presumably to the Invisible.

Ronnie turned to Derek and remarked, "There might be something in what he says."

"He's a fraud, he is," said Derek. "The sort of bloke who does the three-card trick on Oxford Street. Invisible? They know how to make the Queen of Spades invisible."

A well-directed stone hit Derek's helmet.

A gnome appeared from behind a tree, looking pleased at his good shot. Other gnomes appeared, popping up close by. It was time to go. Ronnie and Derek ran for it. Whatever "it" was, they hoped to find "it" somewhere. They hoped to find "it" soon.

6

Ronnie and Derek ran out of the forest. Now, above the treeline, the going was much steeper and harder. But still the malevolent little gnomes pursued them, clambering up the rocks behind them and finding narrow paths.

"I'll blow you up!" Ronnie shouted down at them. The gnomes stopped in their tracks and looked at each other.

"I'll put you in a stew with a lot of dumplings and

eat you!" Ronnie knew the gnomes hated threats. Their pointed ears drooped. They sucked their cap bobbles. They shuffled their feet and dealt them – two to each gnome. Then they were ready to renew the chase.

"I'll put wax in your ears! I'll set fire to your socks! And file your teeth with sandpaper!"

The gnomes stopped again, squeaking and nodding as they consulted with each other. It sounded bad. Then they must have decided they were in such numbers that they could ignore these threats. On they came again, climbing relentlessly towards the two fugitives. Fortunately Derek had used the break in the chase to look round carefully. He had noticed the mouth of a cave. How far it led into the hill he did not know, but it was getting too steep to climb much further outside.

"This way!" he called out, and they ran into the cave. Luckily it was not a dead end, and the track led eventually into huge caverns. When they were deep inside the hill Derek stopped for another breather.

"The acoustics are very good in here," he said. "I should know, I'm in the Police Choir at home." He began singing:

"Your tiny hand is frozen
Let me take it into mine ... "

The gnomes had followed them into the caverns and were immediately bemused by the sound of the song echoing from wall to wall, multiplying Derek's voice. They looked round nervously, trying to identify the whereabouts of a male-voice choir. Ronnie saw a huge boulder that was finely balanced.

He gave it a push. Derek joined him and they shoved together. The boulder rolled down the cavern, gathering speed. The gnomes were still preoccupied, looking for a regimental choir, when the boulder scattered them like ninepins. But, like ninepins, they were soon on their feet again, the right way up, ready to attack.

Ronnie and Derek fled up a smaller tunnel, scrambling and crawling towards the light at the end.

"We're coming out at the other side of the hill," said Derek, puffing mightily. They emerged on to a narrow ledge. Below them was a steep drop, above them a sheer rock face. Behind them were the evil gnomes. They were trapped.

"Now what do we do?" said Derek.

"This is what the Abbot was talking about," replied Ronnie. "Something will turn up, don't worry. From the Invisible."

"Cooeeeee!" came a call, as Mr Dimple sailed into view upon a piece of green carpeting.

"Am I glad to see you," he said. "I found another remnant in the stockroom, so I took it round to your house. It seemed no one was in. I went round the back and found a crumpled-up piece of paper by the dustbins." He produced the piece of paper. "On it was written a word I guessed to be magic. Not believing in such things, I decided to put it to the test. So I stood on the carpet and said it – that magic word – and here I am. One can only conclude that in this world things are not always what they seem … "

Ronnie and Derek leapt into space and landed on the carpet.

"Mind my shopping!" said Dimple. "I had to bring it with me, as I was on my way home. I live on my own. I'm a bachelor. Perhaps I'm a bit stuck in my ways, but that can't be helped … "

The gnomes appeared on the ledge and started throwing rocks at them.

"Oh dear," said Dimple. "You seem to have attracted some very unpleasant company."

"You're right there," said Derek, as he picked up a box of biological washing powder from the shopping. "Is this good with stains?" He passed the box to Ronnie.

"Oh, very good. Use only a little," advised Dimple, "as directed, or you may dissolve your whole wash. It contains an enzyme that attacks all foreign substances."

"That could include gnomes," said Ronnie.

"Precisely," said Derek. "We don't know what sort of plastic they're made of. It's worth a try."

"As long as we save the box tops for the bargain offer," agreed Dimple. "You can win a fortnight's holiday with a sailor of your own choice in Marseilles."

The magic carpeting, responding to the encouraging shouts of Ronnie and Derek, circled once, then swooped upon the ledge, which was now packed with gnomes. Ronnie sprinkled the packet of biological washing powder upon them. For a moment they all wondered whether the mysterious enzyme would work. Then the gnomes began to shrink and sizzle – the plastic bubbling, their grinning faces dissolving, their red cheeks dripping, their beards curling up. Folding, sighing, spitting, they melted into small, smoking puddles.

Thus ended the gnomes.

"Oh, la, la," said Dimple.

"Let's go home," called out Derek.

"MAZAREHSUBLA!" shouted Ronnie.

The magic carpeting flew towards the mountains, out of Shangri-La – a place that once had been and now was no more.

"*Au revoir*, Shangri-La!" cried out Monsieur Dimple, practising his Common Market French, as the carpet sped over the mountains, towards the setting sun.

7

The carpet flew past the sun and out into the galaxy. Through the galaxy it flew, into an army of stars. Past planets, dead worlds, the odd vortex or two of swirling darkness, patches of light, hints of immense distance and the sudden closeness of new blazing suns – past all these flew the carpet. Sometimes the travellers had a sense of movement; at other times they seemed still, while the Universe rushed by. Like a living thing, it wrapped them round, as though digesting them in its coil of moons and stars, planets, worlds and galaxies.

Finally they arrived and they found themselves set down in the hallway of an old house, the magic carpeting still beneath their feet, as though it belonged there. There was a musty smell. Beside them stood an immense grandfather clock, ticking away the seconds of an hour. The clock struck three.

A door opened in the hallway and an elderly man with thick pebble glasses came out.

"I can see you now," he said. He led them into a room full of ticking, tocking clocks, all set at different times. He motioned for Ronnie, Derek and Mr Dimple to sit down, and they did so, gladly.

The old man stared at his visitors, waiting for someone to say something. Time passed – maybe three months, maybe two minutes. It was hard to say, because time was stretched and pinged back like elastic in this room.

"Do you mend clocks?" Ronnie asked at last, gazing round at all the timepieces.

"No, I mend *time*, but I get to it through *clocks*," said the old man. "I can do anything you like with time. Isn't that why you've come here? Do you want it backwards, forwards or sideways? I can do a lot with time. Do you want it up, down or inside out? I'm a Time Mender. Do you want it shortened? Lengthened? Have you got a month that's a bit tight under the arms? Can you get enough into a week? If you want an elephant in a week, I'll have to make it bigger – especially Thursday. I hate untidy weeks that spill out into fortnights. KEEP TIME TIDY, that's what I say. So, what do you want?"

"Can you put the clock back to before my mother bought a piece of flying green carpet?" asked Ronnie.

"I'll have a look. I'm not making any promises," said the old man. "You've left it a bit late – or a bit early – or a bit sideways. Fetch in the grandfather clock in the hall."

Dimple brought in the grandfather clock and set it by the window, where there was more light. Outside, fog obscured the view, or they might have obtained some idea of where they were.

Derek was intent upon furthering his inquiries. As the old man picked up a tool from his work bench, he asked him, "How long have you been mending time?"

"How long's a piece of string, Copper?" snapped back the old man. "You'll find nothing stolen on these premises." He peered into the clock.

"What were you doing before you took up this sort of work?" continued Derek.

"Mind your own business, Bluebottle. I don't have to tell you nuffink … "

"What, not even what planet we're on?" asked Derek.

The old man took a few pieces out of the clock. "No. But I'll tell you something for nuffink,

75

Constable. Once upon a time I made plastic gnomes."

"Did you make them mischievous?" asked Ronnie.

"I don't know if I made 'em mischievous, son. I know I made 'em plastic. Sold 'em off to a garden centre, good riddance."

"Where was this?" persisted Derek.

"Up your nose," said the Time Mender, and one-time Gnome Maker. He returned to the clock, and would say no more.

"Miaou!"

Ronnie looked towards the door and saw a ginger cat.

"That's my cat," he said. "Ginger!" He followed the cat out into the hallway and up the stairs. Along a corridor it went and Ronnie followed. The cat's tail disappeared into a room and Ronnie walked in.

He found Mum and Dad, watching television, upon the piece of flying green carpeting.

"Hello," said Dad. "You're home early from school today, Ronnie."

Mum said, "Hello, Ronnie. We'll have tea soon, dear."

They had no memory of Shangri-La, nor any recollection of how they'd got here. Dad thought it had something to do with not paying the mortgage. That's as far as it went.

Ronnie knew the carpet had brought them here. But what of the others? He ran down the corridor, opening door after door. Inside the rooms, watching TV, were other pairs of specimens from the People Zoo. They were better off in Shangri-La, thought Ronnie. At least they danced every night there.

He ran downstairs and into the Time Mender's room.

"There are a lot of people upstairs," he said.

"That's all right," said the Time Keeper. "The Government pays for them while they're here at the Hotel Cosmic. As long as they don't pinch the light bulbs."

"But why have they all come here?" asked Ronnie.

"It's the carpet that's come here, son. They happened to be on it," observed the Time Keeper, not solving anything.

"But these people were kidnapped by gnomes," explained Ronnie. "I'm trying to help them get home."

"You already have done," said the Time Mender, closing the door of the grandfather clock. "I've put the time back now. Back as you asked, young man. It's a cosmic clock. It's come from space. It's got great influence, so it's true for everyone here. They'll all have to leave now – whether they want to or not – and go back ... "

"Back to where they came from?" asked Derek.

"Not so much 'where' as 'when', Copper. It's beyond your powers of deduction, Narkface."

"There's no need to be so rude," said Derek.

"When can we go?" asked Ronnie.

"Now," said the old man. "And you can take the clock with you as a souvenir."

"Thank you," said Ronnie.

The fog had cleared. Furniture vans were arriving outside the hotel. Ronnie and his parents were among the first to leave. Their furniture, including the grandfather clock, was loaded in the back, not forgetting the cat.

Of course, the carpet remained behind. Yes, it had come home to rest at the Hotel Cosmic – all its magic used up – and now it would be trodden underfoot until the end of its days. Unless – what? Unless a gnome ... But the gnomes had vanished ... or had they?

Ronnie thought the foreman in charge of removals looked suspiciously like the Abbot, and his men looked very much like the Smiling Monks.

"We're going home," said Ronnie.

"You're not going anywhere. It's the scenery that changes around you, that's all," said the foreman (who *definitely* sounded like the Abbot).

It was time to go. Soon everyone would be leaving. They all took the same road away from the Hotel

Cosmic (Aliens Welcome), through blank suburban streets and featureless vistas. It could be Mars, thought Ronnie, if we're in that galaxy.

Suddenly he found that they were driving down his street. How they had got there, he could not remember. The removal van must have dropped off Derek and Dimple along the way, because they were not with them any longer. Perched up in the front of the van with the driver were Ronnie, Mum, Dad and Ginger the cat as they arrived at last outside their house, home again.

The other specimens from the Shangri-La People Zoo were soon home too. One thing they all had in common from their trip – apart, that is, from a completely blank memory and moments of unease if anyone turned the television off – was a passion for ballroom dancing.

When Ronnie woke up the next morning his mother had decided to go to Carpet Kingdom and buy a new fitted carpet for the lounge. He knew they would not buy flying green this time. He would make sure of that.

But Carpet Kingdom had closed down. The gnome outside the car-park entrance had vanished. Ronnie saw Mr Dimple a week later. He had taken a job in a circus.

"Ho, ho, ho," said the clown, when Ronnie asked him if he remembered Shangri-La.

When he saw Derek, now a sergeant, he asked him, "Do you remember Shangri-La?"

"It's a closed case, Ronnie," said Derek. But he winked and murmured under his breath, "It's taught me to trust the Invisible. All the things we touch and see are only clues to that – the Invisible."

The grandfather clock turned out to be very valuable. Dad sold it and paid off all the mortgage arrears. Another stroke of luck was that Dad got a job in a garden centre. If good things come in threes, this was the third: one sunny day Dad came home with a plaster gnome he had been given by the management. As he held it out to Ronnie, it slipped from his hand and smashed into a thousand pieces.

Ronnie smiled. "Go on, make my day," he said to the bits of gnome.